W9-BRN-186

The PRINCESS and the LORD of NIGHT

WRITTEN BY *Emma Bull*

ILLUSTRATED BY
Susan Gaber

JANE YOLEN BOOKS
HARCOURT BRACE & COMPANY
San Diego   New York   London
Printed in Singapore

Copyright © 1994 by Emma Bull
Illustrations copyright © 1994 by Susan Gaber

Library of Congress Cataloging-in-Publication Data
Bull, Emma, 1954–
The princess and the Lord of Night/by Emma Bull;
illustrated by Susan Gaber. — 1st ed.
p.   cm.
Summary: Cursed at birth by an evil lord, a princess
uses intelligence, cleverness, and generosity
to outwit the lord and undo the spell.
ISBN 0-15-263543-2
[1. Fairy tales.] I. Gaber, Susan, ill. II. Title.
PZ8.B8715Pr   1994
398.2—dc20   93-19151   [E]

First edition   A B C D E

The illustrations in this book were done in watercolor
and colored pencil on Strathmore Bristol board.
The display type and text type were set in Centaur
by Thompson Type, San Diego, California.
Color separations were made by Bright Arts, Ltd., Singapore.
Printed and bound by Tien Wah Press, Singapore
Production supervision by Warren Wallerstein
and Ginger Boyer
Designed by Camilla Filancia

This story is for Carolyn Brust,
with best wishes.

— E. B.

For Heather and Larry

— S. G.

nce upon a time there was a princess who had everything she wanted. She had a horse as white as the high clouds of a summer sky who could run from one end of the kingdom to the other in a day. She had a walnut-brown dog who understood anything she said. She had an ash-gray cat as swift as a blink and as clever as six professors. She had a crow as black as the inside of an inkwell who could recite every poem ever written. She had a velvet cloak as blue as twilight that could turn its wearer invisible.

Whenever the princess said she wanted anything — or even when she looked as if she might want something — the king and the queen, her father and mother, hurried to give it to her. For the Lord of Night had put a curse on the princess when she was born, that if ever she wanted something she couldn't have, the kingdom would fall into ruin and the king and queen would die.

Some people, if they got everything they wanted, would become spoiled and silly before they could turn around once. But the princess had seen her mother and father hurrying to get her whatever she wanted, afraid that the Lord of Night might appear in a burst of green smoke and destroy the kingdom if they failed.

The princess felt terrible about it, so she tried to delight in all she had instead of longing for more. Still, there were her horse, and her dog, and her cat, and her crow, and her cloak, which she had wanted and gotten, and she was glad to have them.

On the morning of her thirteenth birthday, the princess woke very early and sat straight up in bed. She had dreamed of something she wanted, and now that she was awake, she found she wanted it more than ever. But she resolved not to tell the king and queen about it. She would go out and get it for herself.

So she mounted her white horse, who could run from one end of the kingdom to the other in a day. She called her brown dog, who understood everything she said. She put her gray cat, swift as a blink and clever as six professors, on the saddle before her. She set the crow who could recite all the world's poems on her shoulder, and tucked the velvet cloak that could make her invisible into the saddle case. Then she rode out into the kingdom to look for what she wanted.

She hadn't been riding for an hour before she met a young man sitting on a stone by the side of the road. He'd covered his face with both hands, and she thought he might be crying.

"What is your trouble?" the princess called to him, from high atop her white horse.

"Oh," he said, looking up at her, "my mother is wasting away with sickness. I have a charm to cure her, but I have to use it before the sun goes down, and she lives far away, on the edge of the sea. I can never reach her in time."

"Well," said the princess, "I want your mother to be well and you to be happy. Take my horse, and you'll be there in time for dinner."

At that, the young man leaped up, full of hope. The princess unstrapped the saddle case and set it on the ground. Then she helped the young man mount the white horse, and watched as they disappeared, fast as the wind, bound for the edge of the sea.

"That's a start to my journey," said the princess, and went on down the road with her dog, her cat, her crow, and the case that held her cloak.

A little farther along the way she entered a forest, and in the forest under a tree she met a ragged, weeping little girl.

"Whatever is the matter?" asked the princess.

"I've lost our sheep," the little girl sobbed, "the ones I was driving to market to sell. They took fright and scattered into the trees. Now I'll have to go home with nothing, and all my brothers and sisters will go cold and hungry."

"That would be a sorry thing," said the princess. "I want you to stop crying, and your family to be well. Here, I shall give you my dog, who understands speech. Tell her to round up all your sheep and help you drive them to market, and she'll do just as you say."

The little girl called to the dog, who bounded up to her. As the princess set off again, she heard the sheep *maaa*-ing and *baaa*-ing as the dog drove them out of the woods.

"I've miles to go yet," the princess said to herself, and went on down the road with her cat, her crow, and her cloak.

She was growing hungry, so when she came to a cottage she decided to stop and ask if anyone there could spare her a bit of bread. When she knocked on the door there was no answer. But she thought she heard a noise inside, so she opened the door and stepped in.

An old woman sat on a stool there, weeping into her apron.

"Why do you weep so, Grandmother?" asked the princess.

"It's the rats!" wailed the old woman. "They've eaten my corn and my oats and my wheat, and tonight they'll finish my barley. And that's all I have to keep me from starving."

"Then dry your tears," the princess bid her. "I want you to be merry, and your larder to be full. So you may have my cat. There's no rat in all the world can outrun or outsmart him. And when I return home, I'll send you corn and oats and wheat to replace what you've lost, and a cow to milk besides."

The old woman leaped up with a shout and threw her arms around the princess. Before she could say "Farewell," the cat had killed three rats and was hunting a fourth.

"One foot in front of the other," the princess said, and went on down the road with her crow and her cloak.

In a little while, she came to a house that stood all alone. There she saw a man sitting on the front step. Tears streamed down his face, but he never made a sound.

"Heavens, what's amiss?" asked the princess.

He shook his head and beckoned her closer. When she put her face down next to his, he whispered, "My poor daughter has fallen under an enchantment. She can neither move nor speak, and the only way to break the spell is to talk to her for three days and three nights. I've talked for a day and a night and half a day, and now I'm so hoarse I cannot talk at all. What can I do to help my girl?"

"I've just the thing," said the princess. "I want your daughter to go free, and you to get your voice back, so I'll give you my crow, who can recite every verse in the world. Just let him perch by your daughter's right hand, and she'll have poems and songs until she can sing them herself."

At that the man flung his hat into the air and took the crow with great delight.

"The path to home's not easy yet," the princess said, and went on down the road, carrying the case that held her cloak that could turn its wearer invisible.

At last she came to a place where the land was hilly, and great
boulders stood all around. It was a strange place and smelled of
magic. As she rounded a bend in the road, she came upon a little
boy sitting on the ground with his face hidden in his arms.

"Are you not well?" asked the princess, but cautiously, because
she knew one should be cautious in such a place.

The boy looked up, and she saw it wasn't a boy at all, but a very small brown man with long pointed ears, and a long, long moustache that reached to his waist, and sharp black eyes in a face as wrinkled as a raisin. "Why do you ask?" he said.

"Because I will help if I can," the princess said.

"No one can help," said the little brown man. "The Lord of Night has stolen away my magic in a box of elder wood, and set a beast to guard it. The beast has six eyes on each side of its head. It never eats and it never sleeps. What can you do about that?"

"I've a score of my own to settle with the Lord of Night," the princess told him, "but if I didn't, I would still give you my cloak, because I want you to have justice. Wrap it around you, and you'll be as invisible as air. Then you may walk past the beast as you please, and take your magic back."

The little man gathered up the velvet cloak and looked long at her with his fierce black eyes. "This is a good favor you've done me," he said, "and I would do one for you. But without my magic, I haven't much."

He pulled a fine gold ring with a blue stone off his thumb. "Still, you may have this from me," said the little brown man. "If you keep the stone turned in, what people tell you will come true. But if you turn the stone out, then promise what they will, everything they say will end up false."

"Thank you very much," the princess replied, "and I'll take care with it."

She blinked, and the little man was gone, because he'd wrapped himself in her cloak.

"Journey's end," the princess said. She put the little man's ring in her pocket and set out home again by the shortest way.

When she reached the palace, her mother and father ran out to meet her.

"Daughter, tell me quickly. Is there anything you want?" the queen asked, full of fear.

"Why do you want to know?" said the princess.

"Because the Lord of Night is here," answered her father the king, "and he says we must give up our kingdom and our lives because the curse has come to pass."

"Oh," said the princess. "Well, tell him if he'd like to know what I want, he'll have to ask me himself. Bring him to me."

The king and queen hurried back to the palace. In a moment, the Lord of Night himself, dressed all in black and with eyes like little flames, came out to meet her. The king and queen followed, their faces pale as milk.

"I think there is something you want," he said, in a voice like wind hissing through dead leaves.

"And what would that be?" asked the princess, as bravely as she could, though she was terrified. She had never before been face-to-face with the Lord of Night.

"Your horse and your dog are gone, and your cat and your crow."

"That they are," the princess answered. "A young man has the horse, a little girl has the dog, an old woman has the cat, and a man and his daughter have the crow." But the princess said nothing about her cloak, because the Lord of Night hadn't.

"I gave the wasting sickness to the young man's mother," the Lord of Night said, cracking his knuckles one by one. "I frightened the little girl's sheep, so that they would all be lost in the forest. I sent the rats to eat the old woman's grain, and I laid the enchantment on the man's daughter so that she could neither move nor speak. I did all that to trap you. I made you give up the things you want."

"That's not true," the princess replied. "I gave away my horse to the young man because I wanted him to save his mother. I gave my dog to the little girl because I wanted her to get her sheep to market. I gave my cat to the old woman because I wanted her to have enough to eat. I gave my crow to the man because I wanted his daughter to move and speak again. And I wanted all of them to be happy. I got just what I wanted."

"It's not so!" cried the Lord of Night. "You want something! You've wanted something since this morning, and haven't got it. I know, I can smell it all around you!"

"Now that," said the princess, "is a fact, and I'll tell you what it is. I want to be free of your curse." And she slipped her hand in her pocket, where she'd put the ring the little brown man had given her.

"Never!" the Lord of Night shrieked. "You'll bear that curse until the end of your life."

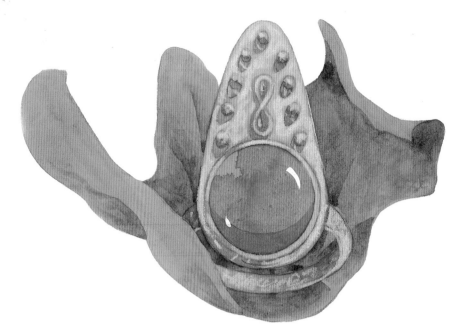

But as he spoke, the princess popped the fine gold ring on her finger and turned the blue stone to face out. Then she took her hand out of her pocket and showed the ring to the Lord of Night.

He stared in dread at the ring with its blue stone sparkling at him like laughter. "Where did you get that ring? Where?" he screamed.

"I think you know where," said the princess, "and I think you know this ring. A little brown man gave it to me, and told me that if I turned it so that the stone faced out, anything said to me would be made false. And that's what I did when you spoke. Now my curse is gone, for you did the uncursing yourself."

"Then the little brown man shall pay for it," vowed the Lord of Night in a fury.

"Will he? But he gave me the ring in return for my cloak that makes its wearer invisible. And if he hasn't used it by now to get his magic back, I'd be surprised."

"No! No!" the Lord of Night howled, and disappeared in a burst of green smoke.

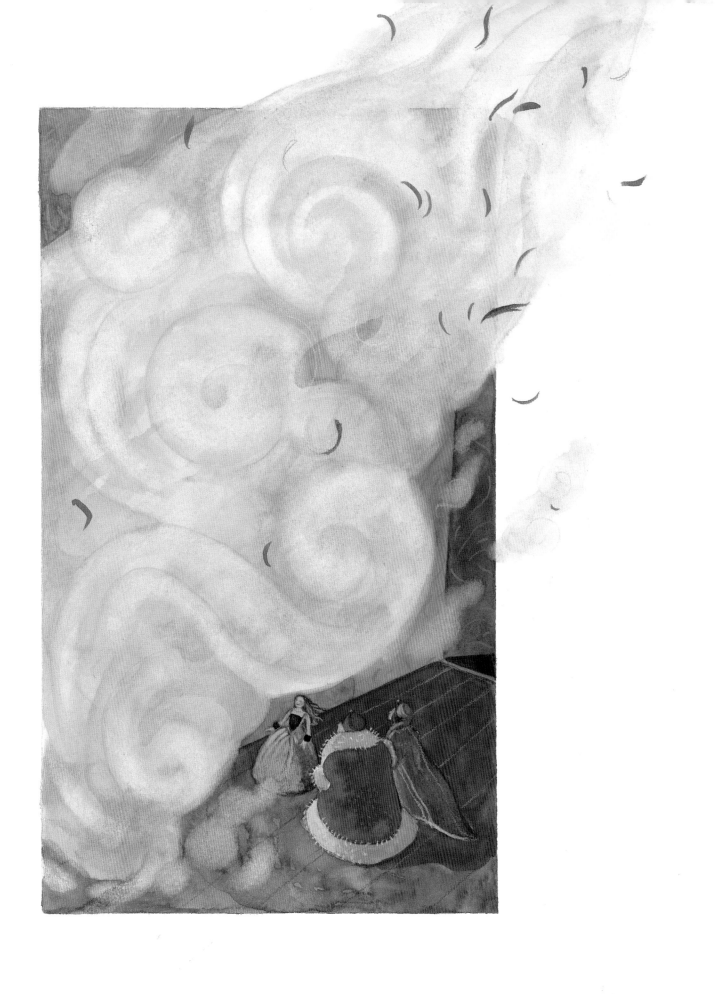

The king and queen were overjoyed. They announced a great celebration to be held the very next night in the palace. The princess invited the young man, the little girl, the old woman, and the man and his daughter.

The young man brought his mother, who was as hale and rosy as if she'd never been sick in her life. The little girl brought her parents and her brothers and sisters, all dressed in handsome new clothes they'd bought with money from selling their sheep. The old woman brought a sweet, spicy cake she'd made from her flour. The man and his daughter danced the night away, and the daughter sang like a flute as she danced.

The princess invited the little brown man, too, but if he was
there, no one saw him. Everyone who came said there had never
been a better party or a better reason to have one, and all of them
lived happily ever after.

DATE			